The Magic School Bus

A SCIENCE CHAPTER BOOK

The Great
SHARK
ESCAPE

A SCIENCE

The Magic School Bus®
CHAPTER BOOK
The Great
SHARK ESCAPE

SCHOLASTIC INC.
New York   Toronto   London   Auckland   Sydney
Mexico City   New Delhi   Hong Kong   Buenos Aires

Written by Jennifer Johnston.

Illustrations by Ted Enik.

Based on *The Magic School Bus* books
written by Joanna Cole and illustrated by Bruce Degen.

ISBN 0-439-20421-6

48 47 46 45 44 43 42 41 40 39 38 37   10 11 12 13 14 15 16/0

Designed by Peter Koblish

Printed in the U.S.A.

The author would like to thank Lisa Mielke, Assistant Director
of Education at the New York Aquarium,
for her expert shark advice.

ꓵNTRODUCTION

Hi, my name is Arnold. I am one of the kids in Ms. Frizzle's class.

Maybe you've heard of Ms. Frizzle. (Sometimes we just call her the Friz.) She is a terrific teacher — but strange. One of her favorite subjects is science, and she knows *everything* about it.

She takes us on lots of field trips in the Magic School Bus. Believe me, it's not called *magic* for nothing!

We never know what's going to happen when we get on that bus.

Ms. Frizzle likes to surprise us, but we can usually tell when she is planning a special lesson — we just look at what she's wearing.

One day, Ms. Frizzle wore this outfit to school. I didn't think too much about it — until I spotted the sharks. That's when I got really worried!

Ms. Frizzle must have noticed. Because she *promised* that the field trip she had planned was the ordinary kind. Do you believe that? Well, let me tell you what happened.

⟩CHAPTER 1

"I want to do killer whales," Tim said.

"I'm thinking about doing squids and octopuses," Wanda said.

We were talking about our science reports. Our class was studying ocean life, and everyone had to pick a topic for a report. Little did we know how we'd be doing our research.

"Mine is going to be about sharks," put in Carlos. "What about you, Arnold?"

"Sea animals make me nervous — especially sharks," I said. "I think I'm going to do some kind of plant, like kelp. It's like seaweed."

Keesha giggled. "Kelp?" she asked. "Don't you think that sounds kind of boring?"

I nodded and smiled. Kelp did sound sort of boring. That's exactly what I liked about it. Ms. Frizzle is a great teacher, but I wouldn't mind it if her science lessons weren't always so exciting.

"Sorry, Arnold," said Tim, "but Ms. Frizzle said our reports are supposed to be about ocean *animals*, remember?"

Unfortunately, Tim was right. I groaned. I'd really been planning to do my report on kelp. Now I'd have to find a nonscary ocean animal to write about. But, naturally, Ms. Frizzle knew just how to help us pick topics.

The adventure began when the Friz walked in wearing a dress covered with all kinds of ocean life. "Good morning, everyone!" she said. "As you know, we're in the middle of our unit on ocean animals. It's time for each of you to choose an animal as the topic of your report. What better way to pick one than by seeing some with your own eyes!"

"Yay, a field trip!" Keesha said.

"Oh, no, not the bus," I moaned. I thought I said it to myself. But Ms. Frizzle must have heard me.

"Don't worry, Arnold," she said. "We're only taking the bus as far as the ocean."

"What are we going to do then?" Dorothy Ann asked.

"Are we going scuba diving?" asked Tim. "I hope we're going scuba diving!"

"We'd better not be going scuba diving," I mumbled.

"Sorry, Tim, I'm afraid that's not in the plan. But we are going to an aquarium by the ocean," said Ms. Frizzle.

"Cool!" yelled Carlos. "I can hardly wait!"

"This is going to be great," I said. An aquarium sounded neat. Not to mention safe. All of the animals would be in tanks. And we would have to get off the bus, so nothing weird could happen.

"I don't know," said Wanda. "Looking at a bunch of fish in a big tank doesn't sound as exciting as most of our field trips."

Ms. Frizzle told Wanda not to worry. "The aquarium has lots more than just fish. After all, the ocean contains about one million species of plants and animals!"

She pulled some thick booklets from her desk drawer. "The director of the aquarium sent these brochures for you. They have oceans of information about underwater life."

From the Blue Water Aquarium's Ocean Brochure

Oceans cover three-quarters of the earth's surface. They are home to about one million species, from tiny one-celled organisms to the world's largest animal, the blue whale. Fish, mammals, reptiles, and lots of other kinds of animals live in oceans.

Actually, the earth has just one big ocean. But it is divided into five main areas that we call the five oceans. You can sail in a boat from one main area to the other areas, because they are all connected.

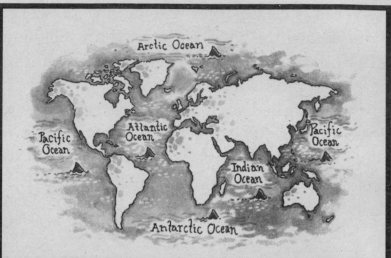

The Pacific Ocean is the biggest and deepest. It's bigger than all the land on Earth put together. It holds almost half of the world's seawater.

The Atlantic Ocean is the second–biggest ocean. It is about half the size of the Pacific.

The Indian Ocean is the third–largest ocean.

The Antarctic (or Southern Ocean) surrounds Antarctica and the South Pole.

The Arctic Ocean surrounds the North Pole. It is the smallest ocean.

"Wow, this is going to be great," Wanda said. "I can't believe there are millions of plants and animals in the oceans!"

"Hey, Ms. Frizzle," Ralphie said. "We're studying sharks next in our ocean unit. Do you think they have a shark at the aquarium?"

"Oh, yes, Ralphie, the aquarium has several types of sharks," Ms. Frizzle said.

"Several *types*," Keesha said. "I didn't know there was more than *one* type of shark."

"Me neither," said Tim. "I thought a shark was a shark."

"Oh, no," the Friz said. "There are hundreds of different kinds of sharks. And they are all very interesting. In fact, some of you may want to choose one kind of shark to write about in your reports."

Sharks, Sharks, Sharks
by Tim

There are 368 known species of sharks! Sharks come in many sizes. A shark can be as small as your hand (the seven-inch spined pygmy shark).

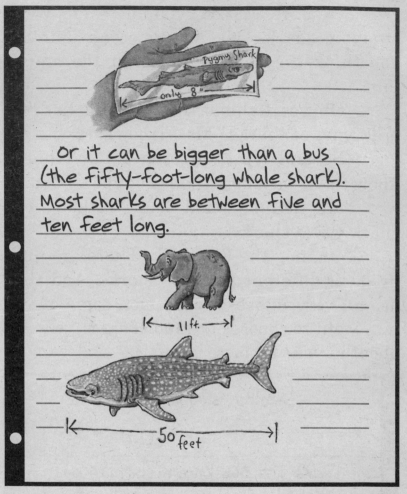

or it can be bigger than a bus (the fifty-foot-long whale shark). Most sharks are between five and ten feet long.

"Ms. Frizzle, what is a shark, anyway?" Wanda asked. "Are sharks related to whales and dolphins?"

From the Desk of Ms. Frizzle

Shark Bits

A shark is a fish. But unlike other fish, sharks do not have bones. Their skeletons are made of a tough material called cartilage. It's the same stuff that's in human noses and ears.

Like other fish, sharks have organs called gills. They use their gills to get oxygen from the water. (Mammals have lungs and get oxygen from the air.) Sharks have five to seven pairs of gill slits on the sides of their heads, while bony fishes have just one pair.

Sharks have many different body types. But most sharks are shaped like torpedoes. Their bodies are made to glide swiftly through the water. Most shark tails are longer on top than on the bottom.

Here's the body of a typical shark:

Classic Shark Shape

"Good question, Wanda," the Friz replied. "Whales and dolphins are mammals — just like people, dogs, cats, bears, and lots of other animals. Sharks are fish, but they aren't exactly like other fish. You'll learn more about sharks when we get to the aquarium. To the bus!"

We all piled into the bus. We've had a lot of wacky adventures in that bus. And even though Ms. Frizzle had promised, I had a feeling this wouldn't be an ordinary ride.

Liz, our class lizard, sat up front with the Friz as she turned on the ignition. Soon, we were on our way to the Pacific Ocean.

⟩CHAPTER 2

The Magic School Bus zoomed along. We looked at our ocean brochures. I hoped to find a nice, friendly-looking sea creature to do my report on. I looked at the brochure's pictures of the aquarium's supersecure shark tanks. But I didn't get any great ideas for my report.

In a little while, Ms. Frizzle drove into a parking lot right beside a sunny ocean beach. I could see the Blue Water Aquarium, too. But there seemed to be a problem.

There was a huge pool of water around the Blue Water Aquarium. Water was leaking out from under all the doors of the building. Trucks with hoses were sucking up the water, but more water kept flowing out.

A tall man with bushy hair and round glasses came splashing toward us from the aquarium. He was wearing a necktie shaped like a fish. The man walked right up to the door of the bus. The Friz opened the door.

"Kids," Ms. Frizzle said, "this is Mr. Hill. He's the director of the aquarium."

"Ms. Frizzle, I'm so sorry," said Mr. Hill. He looked down at his shoes while he talked. "I'm afraid I've got bad news."

"What happened, Mr. Hill?" the Friz asked.

"The dolphins were playing with a rubber ball," Mr. Hill explained. "Somehow it got stuck in a drainpipe in their tank. Anyway, the tank overflowed and the whole aquarium flooded. All of our ocean animals are okay. But we've had to close for the day while we clean up the mess."

"Oh, no!" The whole class groaned. The whole class except for me, that is. Secretly, I was kind of relieved that I wouldn't have to get close to a shark. But I should have known it was just wishful thinking, because that's when Ms. Frizzle got that twinkle in her eye.

"I think I've got a solution to this problem," she said. "Have a seat, Mr. Hill." Ms. Frizzle flipped a few switches on the dashboard of the bus as Mr. Hill climbed aboard.

In a few seconds, we heard a loud whirring noise. Then we felt the bus lift off the ground and rise straight up into the air. The bus had turned into a helicopter.

A look of shock crossed Mr. Hill's face. I knew just how he felt. "What's going on?" he cried.

"Don't worry," I told him with a sigh. "You're on the Magic School Bus — er, Helicopter. This kind of thing happens all the time."

The Magic School Helicopter flew over the beach. Then it headed out over the water. I got a sinking feeling in my stomach.

"Where are we going, Ms. Frizzle?" Phoebe asked.

"You'll see," the Friz replied. In a short while we were way out over the ocean. We couldn't even see land. Suddenly, the helicopter began to go down, toward the water.

Mr. Hill looked as worried as I felt. "Ms. Frizzle? I don't think you can land out here."

"Oh, I'm not landing," said Ms. Frizzle. "Not exactly, anyway." As we hit the water, Liz pushed a few buttons on the helicopter's instrument panel. I closed my eyes. The helicopter hit the water and rocked on the surface for a minute. Then it began to sink. I opened my eyes. The Magic School Helicopter had turned into a Magic School Submarine!

"We're going down deep!" Ms. Frizzle said. Not only was the sub going down deep, it was shrinking and so were we! Now the sub was only two feet long. Everything in the ocean looked huge! "Now that we're smaller we can explore the amazing life of the ocean and see things closer up. We can pretend we're a little fish in a big ocean."

15

"Hey, Ms. Frizzle, there's something fishy about this field trip!" Carlos called out.

"There's something scary about this field trip," I grumbled.

"I think it's going to be fantastic!" Mr. Hill said. He didn't seem upset anymore.

The bus-sub had lots of portholes along its sides. We could see hundreds of fish swimming by — right in front of us! Even I had to admit, it was pretty awesome.

"Excuse me, Mr. Hill," said Ralphie. "Is there any chance we'll see a shark here?"

I could feel my heart beat faster. I really hoped the answer would be no.

"Oh, it's possible," said Mr. Hill. "It's very possible. There are a number of sharks that live in this area."

Oh, great. What was Ms. Frizzle thinking?

No one else seemed alarmed. "Cool!" said Keesha. "We learned that there are over three hundred species of shark. Do they *all* live near here?"

"Oh, no, not all of them," answered Mr. Hill. "Some of them live deeper down in the water. Some of them live in other parts of the Pacific, where the water is cooler. Some don't live in this ocean at all."

They're Everywhere
by Dorothy Ann

You can find sharks all over the world. Sharks live throughout the five main ocean areas and in many seas. They are marine (saltwater) fish. But a few sharks, such as the bull shark, have been known to swim into freshwater rivers and lakes. Bull sharks have been spotted in the Mississippi River in the United States and in the Amazon River in Brazil.

I didn't want to see any sharks at all. But at least I didn't have to worry about seeing all 368 kinds. Well, probably not. On a Magic School Bus field trip, almost anything is possible.

⟩CHAPTER 3

The sub chugged along. Some of the fish we passed were really cool. I actually started to relax a little. A bunch of fuzzy-looking green stuff was floating around us, too.

"Hey, Ms. Frizzle, what is that stuff?" Keesha asked.

"It's called plankton, Keesha," the Friz answered. "It's a mixture of tiny plants and animals. It's one of the basic food sources for fish and other sea creatures."

We were all looking at the plankton when a dark shadow fell over the window. I knew it was bad news. Something huge was on the other side of the glass. We were staring straight into an enormous open mouth! The mouth was filled with thousands of teeth. Up close, they were very small.

A stream of water and plankton was rushing into the giant mouth. And we were right in the middle of the stream.

"Ms. Frizzle! Watch out!" I cried.

Everyone else looked scared, too. "It's going to suck us in!" Wanda cried.

"Hold on tight, everyone!" the Friz said. Just then, Liz punched some controls on the instrument panel with her tail. At the last second, the sub zoomed deeper into the water — we dropped just below the big mouth.

Whew! That was close! But as soon as I thought we were safe, Ms. Frizzle steered the sub so we were right beside a huge shark. We were so close to it that we couldn't see anything else.

What was Ms. Frizzle thinking?

"It's bigger than a semi!" Ralphie said.

"This is a real close encounter," Ms. Frizzle said. "Take a good look."

Even though I was scared, I couldn't help looking. The giant shark had dark gray skin with pale yellow spots and lines all over it.

Mr. Hill had been very quiet since we left the aquarium, but now he looked very pleased. "Kids, that thing is a whale shark."

"A whale shark," said Ralphie. "Is that a kind of shark — or a kind of whale?"

"According to my research, it's the biggest fish in the sea," D.A. said.

Suddenly, the whale shark shut its gigantic mouth. Water rushed out of the gills on the side of its head. The force of the water made the sub start spinning around in circles!

"Don't worry," Mr. Hill said. "It has a huge mouth but it only eats tiny, tiny fish and plankton."

Monster Mouth

by Carlos

A whale shark is a shark, not a whale. It's the biggest fish in the world. It can grow up to fifty feet long and can weigh as much as fifteen tons.

Whale sharks have three thousand tiny teeth. But they don't use their teeth to eat. Whale sharks are filter feeders. They have built-in food filters called gill rakers.

Here is how they work: The whale shark swims with its large mouth open. It sucks in massive amounts of water. Plankton and tiny fish go in with the water. The whale shark pushes the water back out through its gill rakers. But the plankton and other stuff is left behind for dinner. It works like a strainer. A whale shark can filter about fifteen thousand gallons of water an hour!

Four-Inch Thick Skin

Gill Rakers

Five Huge Gill Slits

"Hang on, class," Ms. Frizzle said as we whirled through the water. She quickly got the sub under control and steered us away from the whale shark's head. Then she stopped the sub not far away.

"If that thing is a shark," I asked, "shouldn't we be getting as far away from it as possible?"

"Oh, no," Mr. Hill said. "Now that we're away from its mouth and gills, we're in no danger. In fact, the whale shark is called the gentle giant because it never bothers people."

"But I thought all sharks were dangerous," Wanda said. She looked nervous. She and I seemed to be the only ones who were not crazy about hanging out with a shark.

"Oh, not at all," said Mr. Hill.

"According to my research," said D.A., "only about twenty-five types of sharks are dangerous to people."

"That's correct," said Mr. Hill. "Some sharks *are* dangerous. But most species have *never* attacked people."

From the Blue Water Aquarium's Ocean Brochure

SHARK ATTACK: Get the Facts

- 93% of all shark species are harmless to humans.
- Most shark attacks are caused by people getting too close to sharks and frightening them.
- The great white shark, tiger shark, bull shark, and oceanic white-tip shark are the four sharks most dangerous to humans. They are the most likely to attack without being provoked.
- Sharks attack fewer than one hundred people each year. Very few of those attacks are fatal.
- About two-thirds of all shark attacks take place in cloudy or muddy water. The sharks mistake their human victims for prey animals.

When I looked around the sub, I noticed that everyone's faces looked green.

"I guess I'm not scared of the whale shark anymore," said Wanda. "But I think I'm getting seasick from the waves it's making."

The whale shark was moving its whole body from side to side. It *was* making lots of waves. But they weren't bothering me. I kind of liked riding the waves.

"That's another unique feature of the whale shark," Mr. Hill said. "Most whales mainly use their tails to push themselves through the water. But the whale shark uses its whole body."

"It's not just moving its body — it's moving *my* stomach!" Ralphie said with a worried look on his face.

"I feel a little queasy myself," Ms. Frizzle said. "Liz, full speed ahead!"

❯CHAPTER 4

The bus-sub chugged away from the whale shark. Maybe that shark was a gentle giant, but I was glad to escape it.

Carlos wasn't so glad. In fact, he liked that gigantic shark so much that he decided to do a report on it.

I watched fish out of one window for a while. I still didn't know what my report would be about. I hoped the perfect topic would just float by. Then I turned to look out another window. That's when I discovered a much bigger worry. I could see something heading toward us. It looked like — *oh, no*! It looked like another shark.

This shark was gray and shaped like a torpedo. It was much smaller than the whale shark — and a lot faster! It was gliding toward us at lightning speed. Only its tail moved. One thing was for sure. This shark was no gentle giant.

"Ms. Frizzle!" I screamed. "Help! Shark! Help!"

"Oh, bad! Oh, bad! Oh, bad!" Keesha yelled. "Arnold, that looks like a great white!"

"Cool," Ralphie said. "Now I'll have first-hand information for my report."

Super Predator

by Ralphie

Great white sharks are the most feared sharks in the ocean. The great white is a fierce hunter. It gets its name for its white belly. The great white's top is gray, which helps it blend into the dark water and sneak up on prey.

The great white has razor-sharp, triangle-shaped teeth. But it doesn't use its teeth for chewing. It uses them to rip into its prey and then it swallows the pieces whole. Adult great white sharks go after sea lions, seals, otters, sea turtles, and even some kinds of whales.

Great White Shark

"A great white!" shouted D.A. "That's one of the most dangerous sharks in the world!" Suddenly, everyone in the sub seemed as scared as I was.

"Hey, wha-what's it doing?" Wanda asked.

The great white was arching its back.
Then it threw back its head. Unfortunately, I
got a very good look at its enormous white teeth.

Even Mr. Hill looked panicked. "Ms.
Frizzle!" he said. "The great white only moves
its back and head like that when it's going to
attack. This one looks ready to take a bite out
of us. We've got to do something!"

"Never fear," Ms. Frizzle said. "The
Magic School Sub will take us out of here!"
She pulled a lever on the sub. We plunged

It's a great white!

What's so great about it?

downward, deeper into the ocean — just in time to escape the jaws of the great white. It swam past us over our heads.

"Whew, what a relief!" Ralphie said.

"Did you see all those teeth?" Phoebe asked.

"According to my research, the great white shark has five rows of teeth," D.A. informed us.

"Wow. Just imagine the dental bills!" Carlos said.

"Actually, sharks lose teeth all the time," Mr. Hill told him. "But new teeth always come in to replace the ones that fall out."

"I'll remember that for my report," Keesha said.

Sharks Don't Need Dentists
by Keesha

Sharks can have as many as three thousand teeth at one time.

Sharks lose teeth pretty often, sometimes every day. Then the lost teeth are replaced with new ones. Here's how that works:

Most sharks have five rows of teeth. They use the first two for catching prey. When one of these front teeth is lost, a replacement tooth moves forward from one of the back rows. Then a new tooth comes in to fill the space in the back row.

>CHAPTER 5

The bus-sub kept dropping downward. It felt like we would keep falling forever.

"That was a close call," Ms. Frizzle said. "Let's bump the bus back up to full size and explore more ocean life!"

"Can we go home before we explore more ocean life?" I asked hopefully.

"No way," Ralphie said. "The ocean is awesome."

"Don't worry, Ralphie," Ms. Frizzle told him. "This field trip isn't over yet."

"Yay!" Ralphie shouted.

Ugh, I thought. I knew it. And I still hadn't found a report topic.

"We're on our way to the bottom of the ocean," the Friz continued.

"Don't look so nervous, Arnold," Mr. Hill said to me. "The ocean's not very deep here. The floor's only three hundred feet down."

Only? I thought.

"Hey, Liz, *floor* it!" Carlos shouted.

"Hey, I think I can see the ocean floor," Keesha said.

There was a small window in the floor of our sub. I looked through it. Sure enough, I could see the sandy, golden-brown bottom beneath us. But all of a sudden, it started to move.

"Wh-wh-whoooaa!" Ralphie shouted.

"Ms. Frizzle, what's going on?" Tim asked. "That sand is moving around!"

Ms. Frizzle put the engine in reverse just in time to stop us from landing on the shifting sand. Just then, something long, flat, and wide wiggled its way free of the sand and swam off!

Mr. Hill chuckled. "It wasn't the ocean floor that was moving!" he exclaimed. "It was an angel shark. Its flat body and sandy-colored skin allow it to bury itself in the sand and blend right in."

"According to my research," D.A. said, "when an animal blends in with its surroundings that way, it's called camouflage."

"Very good, D.A.," Ms. Frizzle said. "Camouflage is exactly what it's called. It

helps the animal to sneak up on prey — and to hide from predators."

"That makes sense," Ralphie said. "But this time, that angel shark's camouflage almost got it crushed by a Magic School Sub!"

"I'm going to do my report on angel sharks," Phoebe said.

Angel Shark

by Phoebe

The angel shark has a flat body. It gets its name from its long, wide fins that look like wings. Angel sharks are bottom-dwellers. They bury themselves in the sand or mud with only their eyes and part of their bodies showing. Angel sharks live in the Pacific Ocean. They are often caught by other sharks for food.

Angel Shark

"Um, Ms. Frizzle?" I asked. "Are you taking us home now?"

"Not just yet, Arnold," the Friz said. "Not everyone has a report topic. I'm also afraid that sudden reverse did some damage to our Magic School Sub."

Just great. Now we were trapped in the deep blue ocean *and* I still had to find a report topic. But Ms. Frizzle wasted no time. She slid back a panel on the wall of the sub. There was a small closet behind the panel. "Luckily, the sub is equipped with wet suits and air tanks," Ms. Frizzle said. "We'll all put these on so we can go out and do some repairs."

Ms. Frizzle took the stuff out of the closet. There was even a tiny air tank for Liz. Everyone began getting dressed.

"The wet suits have cables attached to them," said Ms. Frizzle. "As soon as you swim out the door, hook your cable to the side of the sub."

I groaned. "I knew I should have stayed home today."

"Don't worry, Arnold," Carlos said. "This

will be really cool. You can always stay home tomorrow."

I hoped he was right. At this rate, I wasn't sure if we'd be home by tomorrow. But I let Carlos help me into my suit and tank. Then I followed him out the door of the sub.

Ms. Frizzle and the others were already out there. I found my cable and attached it to a hook on the side of the sub. Outside the sub, it was quiet and eerie. I saw crabs and lobsters scuttling around on the ocean floor.

Mr. Hill pointed to some tiny bubbles coming up from the sand. "There are clams under there," he said. "All the animals you see down here can be dinner for the bottom-dwelling sharks."

The Friz was busy checking out the sub's engine. "There's something stuck in the motor. It's just a little jammed," she told us.

"I'm glad it's just jammed and not jelly-fished," Phoebe said.

Ms. Frizzle and some of the kids worked to fix the motor. The rest of us looked around.

That's when I got this haunting feeling. Before I knew it, a long, silent, scary form was swimming toward me. It looked like some kind of shark — or the ghost of one! Its skin was a pale pinkish-white. And it had a long, pointy blade sticking out of its upper jaw. I was so nervous I couldn't move.

"Ms. Frizzle!" Wanda shouted. "There's something weird headed toward Arnold!"

I could see everyone turn and look. The thing opened its mouth. My life flashed before my eyes. I was sure this was the end.

Then the shark attacked my cable with its pointy teeth. I wanted to scream, but I was too scared. Then, suddenly, it just swam away. I couldn't believe how lucky I was. I looked around — and realized I wasn't all that lucky. The shark had bitten right through my cable. I wasn't attached to the sub anymore and I was starting to drift far away.

"Help me, you guys!" I shouted. I started to float upward. I couldn't stop!

Then I felt a tug on what was left of my

cable. "Don't worry, Arnold," D.A. called. "We've got you!"

D.A. and Tim reeled me in like a fish. What a relief.

"Thanks, guys," I said.

"What *was* that thing?" Ralphie asked.

Mr. Hill looked very excited. "That was a goblin shark! We were very lucky to see one! Goblin sharks aren't often found in waters this shallow."

"Some luck," I groaned.

"Goblin sharks are rarely seen by people," Mr. Hill went on. "For one thing, they usually hang out much deeper in the ocean."

"You know what, Arnold?" Tim said. "The goblin shark might make a good topic for your report. You got a much closer look at one than most people ever will!"

"No way!" I answered. "I already know way more about goblin sharks than I ever wanted to learn."

"Great," Tim said, "then I'll do *my* report on it."

Spooky Shark

by Tim

The pinkish-gray goblin shark is as pale as a ghost. It has tiny eyes and a long, flat, pointy snout. Some people say it's the world's ugliest shark!

Goblin sharks are as mysterious as ghosts, too. Most of them live way at the bottom of the ocean, in parts of the Atlantic, Pacific, and Indian Oceans. Goblin sharks are hardly ever seen by humans. Even shark experts don't know much about them.

The goblin shark eats shrimp, squid, and various fish — including other sharks.

Goblin Shark

That was fine by me, but I was a little worried about my report. What was I going to write about? It seemed like we'd been underwater forever, and I still hadn't picked a topic.

"Arnold, I'm glad you're back safe," said the Friz. "I'm also glad to announce that Phoebe and Carlos helped me fix the motor. The Magic School Sub is ready to roll. To the sub!"

✦ CHAPTER 6

Back inside, Liz helped us stow our diving gear, while the Friz brought the engine back up to speed. Soon the sub was chugging back toward the surface.

"That goblin shark was really weird-looking," Tim said. "Do any other sharks look like that?"

"No other shark looks exactly like a goblin shark," Mr. Hill told us. "But there are many strange-looking sharks in the sea. Take the thresher shark, for example. Its caudal fin is as long as the rest of its body."

"Caudal fin?" asked Wanda. "What's a caudal fin?"

"That's another name for the shark's tail," Mr. Hill explained.

"So the thresher shark's got a tail that's as long as its body?" Carlos asked. "Sounds like a tall tail to me!"

"And there's the hammerhead," Keesha said.

"Yes, the hammerhead is also very strange-looking," Mr. Hill agreed.

"No, I mean, *there's* the hammerhead — right there!" Keesha shouted. She pointed to the dome of the bus-sub.

A big gray shark was swimming over us. Its body looked like a normal shark's body. But its head was flat and really wide. Big knobs stuck way out on either side of the shark's head — a lot like the top of a hammer.

"We'd better not get too close," said Mr. Hill. "The hammerhead has been known to attack when disturbed. Who knows what it might think of a Magic School Sub?"

"Don't worry, we'll keep our distance," said Ms. Frizzle. "But the hammerhead is an amazing sight, isn't it, class?"

Okay, it was an amazing sight. But I think I'd rather see it on TV or something.

"Hey, what's that next to the hammerhead?" Ralphie asked.

Big Head
by Ralphie

The average hammerhead shark is about eleven feet long. It is easily identified by its superwide head. The hammerhead's eyes are at either end of its head, giving it great binocular vision.

Hammerheads eat fish, squid, octopuses, crustaceans, and other sharks. They've even been known to eat other hammerheads.

Hammerhead Shark

A much smaller shark was swimming beside it. Its head was also a weird shape. But it was not nearly as big as the hammerhead's.

"I'll bet that's a baby hammerhead," Phoebe said.

A Shark Is Born
by Phoebe

Where do baby sharks come from? All sharks' eggs are fertilized inside the mother's body. Some sharks then lay their eggs in a sac on the bottom of the ocean. Later, baby sharks hatch from the eggs. But most sharks' eggs hatch inside their mother's body, and they come out as live babies.

One litter of sharks can include anywhere from 2 to 135 babies. Shark mothers do not take care of their babies.

Shark babies are able to swim and hunt as soon as they are born. They are on their own from day one. Baby sharks face the danger of being eaten by predators, including adult sharks or other baby sharks — gray nurse sharks eat their own brothers and sisters while still inside their mother's body!

"Baby sharks don't hang out with their mothers after they're born," Mr. Hill said. "Actually, that shark is a small species of hammerhead called a bonnethead. Even though it's small, it's an adult shark."

"If that bonnethead were any smaller, the big hammerhead would probably be snacking on it!" Ms. Frizzle told us.

"Really?" asked Carlos. "I guess the ocean's just a shark-eat-shark world, huh?"

"Well, it depends," admitted Ms. Frizzle. "Most shark species are pretty picky about what they eat. Only certain species like hammerheads, great whites, and tiger sharks will eat other sharks."

> ## Time for Dinner
> ### by Carlos
>
> All sharks are carnivores (flesh eaters). But different kinds of sharks have different diets.
>
> Some sharks are fast-swimming predators. They eat fish, squid, seabirds, other sharks, and marine mammals.
>
> Some sharks are slow-swimming predators. They crush and eat shellfish — such as crabs, lobsters, and clams — on the ocean floor.
>
> A few sharks are filter feeders, like the whale shark. Filter feeders just eat krill, plankton, and tiny fish.

The sub moved along and climbed closer to the surface.

"Look, dolphins!" Wanda cried. A pod of dolphins was swimming near us. We watched them through the dome. They took turns leaping out of the water and diving back in. It looked like they were having fun.

"That's awesome!" Carlos said.

But I felt butterflies in my stomach. "What about that hammerhead?" I asked. "I can still see it over there. What if it swims

Look at the hammerhead!

over here and gets the dolphins? And maybe gets us for dessert."

"Relax, Arnold," Tim said. "I don't think the hammerhead even knows the dolphins are here."

D.A. spoke up. "According to my research, that can't be true," she said. "Sharks have incredibly keen senses."

From D.A.'s Notebook
Sensory Overload

Sharks have amazingly sharp senses. If you could experience the world the way a shark does, it would probably blow you away!

A shark's ears can hear a fish struggling from more than a mile away. A shark can also detect sound and movement using its lateral line system. That's a system of pores along the side of a shark's body. It's sort of like the shark can hear with its skin!

Sharks have really good eyesight and an incredible sense of smell, too. Some sharks can smell one drop of blood in one million drops of seawater!

Along with the usual five senses, sharks also have the ability to sense the electrical impulses that animals give off when their muscles contract. This sense helps bottom-dwelling sharks find prey that is hidden in the sand.

"D.A.'s right," Mr. Hill said. "I'm sure the hammerhead is aware of the dolphins. But it may be afraid to take them on."

"Afraid?" asked Ralphie. "Why would a *shark* be afraid of dolphins?"

"You'd be surprised, Ralphie," the Friz answered. "Dolphins have been known to gang up on a shark and hurt it, or even kill it."

Dolphin Defense
by Wanda

You might not think a dolphin could beat a shark in a fight — but you'd be wrong. Dolphins have really tough, strong snouts. A group of dolphins can actually kill a shark. The dolphins can swim beneath the shark and use their snouts to ram its soft belly over and over. This is more likely to happen in a lab or research center than in the ocean. In the wild, dolphins and sharks usually leave one another alone.

The sub cruised forward. Things looked good — for a second. All I needed was a topic for my report, and we could get back to the land. But, all of a sudden, we were surrounded by sharks! It was a whole school of dark blue sharks, all almost exactly alike.

"Throw her into idle, Liz!" Ms. Frizzle shouted.

"Stop?" asked Wanda. "Don't you mean, 'Get us out of here'?"

"It's too late for us to turn away," the Friz explained. "We're already in the middle of their turf."

"That means that the best thing to do is be good guests," Mr. Hill said. "We need to stay still and let them check us out."

"Chances are, they'll just swim away," Ms. Frizzle told us.

I didn't want to know what would happen if they didn't.

"In the meantime, get a close look," Ms. Frizzle told us. "These blue sharks are unusual because they swim in schools like this."

Wolves of the Sea
by Phoebe

Blue sharks are really dark blue. Often, the blue shark is a loner who travels by itself. But you might hear blue sharks called the "wolves of the sea" because they sometimes form large packs, especially when there is food around. Blue sharks sometimes form schools (packs) with other blue sharks that are the same size. And their schools are always all-male or all-female. No one knows for sure why they do this.

The blue shark is a game fish, which means that people fish for it and eat it. Right now, the blue shark is threatened because of overfishing.

Blue
Shark

"Also, their population is shrinking," Mr. Hill added. "Someday, there may not be any more blue sharks to see."

"I'm not so happy to see *these* blue sharks," said Phoebe. "But it would be really sad if the whole species disappeared."

Human Attack!
by Wanda

Can humans be dangerous to sharks? Definitely! Sharks kill only a few people every year. But people fish millions of sharks from the oceans. Some people catch sharks to make shark steak and other kinds of food, oils, and medical uses. But some people don't like sharks and will kill any shark they can catch, even if they have no use for it. Sharks grow slowly, live a long time, and don't reproduce at a high rate. So they are easily threatened by overfishing.

A few of the blue sharks swam right up
to the sub. I held my breath. But the sharks
only looked at us. Then, as Ms. Frizzle had
predicted, they all swam away.

"Okay, class," Ms. Frizzle said. "We're
out of here!"

Boy, was I glad to hear those words. I
crossed my fingers and hoped that we were
going home.

But then I heard the bad news.

"We're headed home just as soon as

everyone picks a topic for their report," the Friz said. "And I think this tiger shark will give you lots of ideas!" Then everything happened fast. The Friz reached for the control panel. Suddenly, I felt myself getting smaller and smaller. The bus-sub was shrinking, and so was everyone inside it. In seconds, the whole sub was no bigger than a small fish.

As I looked out the front window I saw a striped shark right in front of us — its mouth was open wide.

"Hang on tight, class! We're going in!" Ms. Frizzle shouted.

Whoa! Did the Friz mean we were actually going *inside* the shark? This wasn't a field trip — it was a nightmare!

CHAPTER 7

"Down the hatch we go!" Ms. Frizzle shouted. She pulled some levers and drove the bus-sub right past the shark's huge teeth, down its throat, and all the way into its stomach!

That's when Phoebe spoke up. "At my old school, we were never a tiger shark's lunch — or dinner!" she said.

Phoebe was right. We'd been on weird field trips before. But this was out of control. I had to pick a report topic or we'd never get home.

The whole class looked nervous — we were in a shark's stomach!

"Don't worry, kids," Ms. Frizzle said. "We can go right back out the way we came in."

"The tiger shark is sometimes called the 'trash can with fins,'" Mr. Hill informed us. "Look around its stomach and see if you can figure out why."

I didn't really care why. I just wanted to get out of there. But I needed to do a report, so I looked around, anyway.

"I see a crab!" Ralphie said.

"Look over there!" Keesha shouted. "That's the skeleton of a bony fish."

"Hey, there's a turtle shell," Phoebe said. The turtle shell was cool-looking. But I didn't want to think about what had happened to the rest of the turtle.

"Whoa, what's that thing?" I pointed at a fish that was about the same size as our sub. It was shaped like an ordinary fish. But it was glowing like a little flashlight.

"Wow!" Carlos said. "He glows with the flow! How does he do that?"

"That fish is called a flashlight fish," Mr. Hill replied. "Actually, it's not the fish itself that glows. Underneath each eye, the fish has a pouch full of millions of glowing, microscopic bacteria. Some fish are bioluminescent because they use it as a device for mating. The glow helps mating fish find one another."

Living Light
by Carlos

Creatures that glow in the dark are called bioluminescent, which means "living light." Bioluminescence is caused by a chemical reaction. It's the same reaction that makes fireflies and lots of other creatures glow. Bioluminescence is found in species of bacteria, algae, fungi, and invertebrate animals.

"Hey, you guys, check it out," Tim called. "There's an *overcoat* right over there."

"What's that doing in here?" Phoebe asked.

"Well," said the Friz, "I'm not sure how or where this shark found that coat. But I'm not surprised that it decided to eat the coat."

"This tiger shark is one huge garbage disposal!" D.A. said.

Trash Can of the Sea
by Keesha

The tiger shark gets its name from the stripes on its dark back. But it gets its nickname from its eating habits. Tiger sharks will try to eat just about anything.

Tiger sharks travel alone and they are always on the move. A tiger shark may travel as many as fifty miles per day, stopping only to eat. Tiger sharks never go looking for people, but they sometimes attack humans who come near them.

Tiger Shark

"All right, class," Ms. Frizzle said. "Fasten your seat belts. We're going right back up the hatch! Pay special attention to the tiger shark's teeth on your way out."

The tiny sub zipped through the shark's mouth. Unfortunately, I got a close look at its teeth on the way out. They were pointy in the front. In the back, they had tiny edges like a saw. "They don't look like the goblin shark's teeth," I said. "Those teeth were really long and pointy."

"Yes, and the great white shark had teeth shaped like triangles," Phoebe said.

"Very good, Arnold and Phoebe!" Ms. Frizzle said. "Tim, why do you think different sharks have such different teeth?"

"Hmm. Maybe it's because they all eat different foods," Tim replied.

"Excellent, Tim!" Mr. Hill said. "That's exactly why."

Sink your Teeth in

by Tim

The size and shape of a shark's teeth depend on its diet.

Sharks that go after big prey, such as the great white, have flat, triangular teeth with serrated (sawlike) edges. Their teeth are good for cutting off chunks of prey.

for cutting

Great White Shark's Tooth

Some sharks hunt small fish that they can eat whole. These sharks have long, narrow teeth for spearing the small fish.

Mako Shark's Teeth

for spearing

Older teeth snap off

Jaw Cartilage

for crushing

for stabbing

Bullhead Shark's Jaws

Some sharks eat mostly shellfish that live on the ocean

floor. They have teeth that are good for crushing the hard shells of their prey.

Some sharks, like the goblin shark, have spearing teeth in front and crushing teeth in the back.

Scavengers, like the tiger shark, will eat almost anything. They have different kinds of teeth to catch many different types of prey.

Tiger Shark's Tooth for slicing

I thought Ms. Frizzle would unshrink the sub — and us — as soon as we escaped the tiger shark's body. But she got busy talking to Mr. Hill and did not hit the switch that would return us to our normal size.

Then I saw something scary-looking swimming our way. It was flat, and it had a strange shape — it almost looked as if it had wings. A long, skinny tail, like a whip, trailed behind it. And it was big — at least ten or fifteen times the size of our shrunken sub.

"Wh-what *is* that thing?" Keesha asked.

Mr. Hill looked out the window. "Oh, dear," he answered. "That's a stingray! We must be careful not to startle it. Its tail is covered with thorns and it's also got a poison stinger."

"Is it going to get us?" Wanda asked.

"I think we'd better move away from it, just to be safe," Mr. Hill answered.

The Ray Report
by Carlos

Rays are flattened fish that are close relatives of sharks. In fact, scientists believe rays evolved from sharks. Like sharks, rays have no bones, only cartilage.

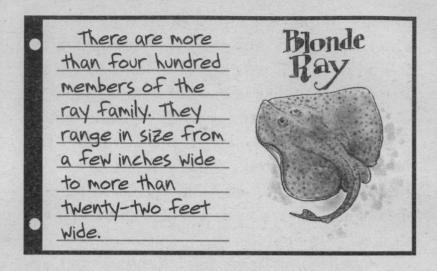

There are more than four hundred members of the ray family. They range in size from a few inches wide to more than twenty-two feet wide.

Blonde Ray

"Full speed ahead, Liz!" Ms. Frizzle shouted. "Hang on tight, class."

Liz pulled a lever on the instrument panel. The tiny bus-sub zoomed forward.

Bad move! The sudden noise and movement seemed to upset the stingray. It zoomed after us at lightning speed. The bus-sub moved fast. But the ray was faster. I just knew we were going to get stung by that tail.

Then Ralphie yelled, "Ms. Frizzle, help! Look at that!"

"It's a shark, Ms. Frizzle! It's coming right at us!" Keesha added.

I looked out the window. A blue-gray shark was swimming toward us — fast. It was going faster than any shark I'd ever seen. And I had seen a lot of sharks by then! I could see that there was something really weird about *this* shark — it was covered with little fish.

"Oh, great, another shark," I groaned. "That's exactly what we need."

"You're right, Arnold!" the Friz said. "That's a mako shark and it *is* exactly what we need — to escape the stingray. Hang on, class. It's time for Operation Remora!"

Operation Re-WHAT-a? I had no idea what the Friz was talking about. But when that shark caught up to us, I saw. Ms. Frizzle did not try to escape it. Instead she pushed a button on the sub's instrument panel. A little suction cup shot out from the sub — and latched right onto the shark.

From the Desk of Ms. Frizzle

Speed Racer

The shortfin mako shark is the fastest shark in the ocean. Some experts say makos have been known to reach speeds of over sixty miles an hour. (The average shortfin mako probably can't swim quite that fast, though.) Makos can leap above the surface of the water, too.

Makos like to eat fish that travel in schools — like tuna, herring, mackerel, and swordfish. But in a pinch, a mako will eat almost anything.

Makos have been known to attack humans. Some humans hunt makos. They are prized as game fish.

Mako Shark

"What are you *doing,* Ms. Frizzle?" Ralphie asked.

"We're hitching a ride out of here," Ms. Frizzle answered. "This mako shark will outswim that stingray!"

"But is this safe?" Wanda wondered.

"It's much safer than getting stung by a ray!" Ms. Frizzle replied. "Do you see the little fish all around us? The shark just thinks we're one of them!"

"What *are* those fish?" asked Tim.

"They're called remoras," Mr. Hill answered. "They often hitch rides on sharks. The sharks rarely bother them."

"Look," D.A. said. "Their fins are like little suction cups, holding them onto the shark's body."

"Whoooaaaa! What's happening?" Ralphie screamed.

"Hang on, everyone!" Ms. Frizzle shouted.

Suddenly, we felt the sub rushing upward. And then — for the first time in *hours* — I saw the blue sky. But only for a second. The mako shark had leaped above the surface. Then it splashed back into the water with a jolt!

"Ohhhh . . ." Keesha moaned. "That made my stomach feel funny!"

"Mine, too," Carlos said.

"Well, look out, because here we go again!" Mr. Hill warned us.

Once again, the mako shark leaped above the surface of the water. It made another leap — and then another and another. I looked around the sub. The other kids' faces were green. So were Mr. Hill's and Ms. Frizzle's. They were all moaning and groaning. Everyone was seasick — except me. I felt just fine. In fact, I thought the leaping was cool. Riding in the Magic School Remora-sub was really fun — and it gave me a great idea for my report!

More About Remoras
by Arnold

The remora, or suckerfish, is a little fish with a suction-cup-like fin. Remoras often use these fins to latch onto sharks and other sea animals. No one is sure exactly why they do it.

Sometimes remoras eat scraps of a shark's meal. But that doesn't seem to be the reason they latch onto sharks. Remoras also hitch rides with creatures that don't eat anything remoras eat.

Some scientists say that remorus are attracted by movement. Instinct tells the remoras to latch onto moving objects.

Sharks have been known to eat remoras, but not very often.

Remora

The mako jumped again. While we were out of the water, I saw that we were close to shore. Awesome! We could finally go home!

"Hey, Ms. Frizzle!" I shouted. "I just saw the shore. I think it's time to detach the sub from the shark."

But Ms. Frizzle didn't answer. She still looked green. She was holding her stomach. She seemed to be too sick to say anything.

What were we going to do? At any minute, this shark might take us back out into the ocean. There was *no way* I was letting that happen. We had had enough close calls. I wanted to get as far from the ocean as possible. I had never been in charge before, and I didn't think I would like it. But it was up to me to get us out of there.

I made my way over to the sub's instrument panel. I felt nervous looking at all those buttons. What if I pressed the wrong one? Then I saw a button marked SUCTION CUP. That had to be the right one. Right?

Nervously, I pressed it. With a pop, the

sub detached from the shark's body. Hooray! We were free!

Now I had to get us to the shore. I took a deep breath and grabbed the wheel. I had never steered a bus-sub before and I wasn't sure if I could do it. But I had been watching the Friz steer all day long. And of course, I'd seen her steer the Magic School Bus lots of times. So I aimed the sub for the beach and tried my best to steer the way Ms. Frizzle did.

Everything went smoothly until we got close to the beach. That's when I realized — in my hurry to get out of there, I was going way too fast! Just when I thought we'd crash into the beach, the sub turned back into a bus and rolled onto the shore. I slammed my foot on the brakes just in time to avoid a crash landing. I couldn't believe my lucky break. We were finally safe on the shore — and it was me, Arnold, who got us there!

After a few minutes on land, Ms. Frizzle and my classmates stopped looking so green. When everyone felt well enough, Ms. Frizzle took the wheel of our normal-sized school bus, and we were on our way home. All the way there, other kids kept telling me I was a hero and talking about how brave I was.

"You know what?" I told Ms. Frizzle. "This turned out to be a pretty cool field trip. But I'd never want to do it again."

"Good old Arnold," Ms. Frizzle said. "I knew we could count on you."

CHAPTER 8

When I walked into the classroom the next day, I got a big surprise. I usually don't like surprises, but this one was awesome. The Friz had planned a "hero's welcome" for me. All of the other kids had gotten to class early. When I walked in, they jumped up and yelled, "Hooray for Arnold!"

Then Keesha stepped up to me. "This is for you, Arnold. We all want to thank you for saving us yesterday!"

She handed me an enormous thank-you card, signed by all the kids in my class. Some of the kids had drawn pictures of sharks on the card. And Tim had drawn a picture of me steering the sub.

"Wow, thanks, you guys," I said. "This is great."

"No, thank *you,* Arnold," D.A. said. "We were all so seasick. We might still be attached to that shark."

"Or inside its stomach!" Wanda added.

Then Ms. Frizzle said, "I've got something for you, too, Arnold. Please step up to the front of the room!"

I walked to the front of the classroom. Ms. Frizzle reached into her desk drawer and handed me a plaque. It said TO ARNOLD, OUR HERO across the top. And it had a picture of a fish drawn on it.

"I'm presenting this to you, Arnold, to thank you for your bravery. But this plaque has a special feature I'd like everyone to see. To the closet, class!"

Our whole class piled into the classroom closet, and Ms. Frizzle turned off the light. The fish picture glowed in the dark. It was just like one of those flashlight fish!

"Arnold, this is for you," Ms. Frizzle said, "because you are a glowing example!"

And you know what? I was really glad I didn't stay home the day of that field trip!

Sharks of the World

On this adventure, we found out a lot about whale, great white, goblin, blue, tiger, and mako sharks. There are many other kinds of sharks. Here are a few of them.

Lemon Shark
by Phoebe

The lemon shark gets its name from its deep yellow back. (Its belly is off-white.) Lemon sharks are usually eight to ten feet long. They have long, sharp teeth for catching slippery fish. Lemon sharks are common on the southeast coast of the United States.

Spined Pygmy Shark
by Arnold

The spined pygmy shark is among the smallest sharks in the world. It is only seven to eight inches long on average. Spined pygmy sharks are dark gray or black on top. Their bellies glow in the dark. These sharks live very deep in the water (down to 6,500 feet) but they migrate up to about 650 feet at night, to hunt. Spined pygmy sharks are harmless to humans.

Spined Pygmy Shark

Nurse Shark
by Ralphie

Nurse sharks are bottom-dwellers. They range in size from seven to thirteen feet. They are dark gray-brown on top and sometimes have spots. They are very sluggish and are harmless unless bothered.

Nurse Shark

Spiny Dogfish Shark
by Keesha

The spiny dogfish shark is the most common shark. It is used by people for food, fertilizer, leather hide, and pet food. It is also studied in research labs more than any other shark. Spiny dogfish sharks live mostly on the bottom in temperate or subarctic waters. They are dark gray with white spots and white bellies. Spiny dogfish sharks eat fish, squid, and octopus. They are called dogfish sharks because, like some blue sharks, they hunt and travel in packs. They are also called dogfish sharks because, like dogs, they are very common.

Spiny Dogfish Shark

Join my class on all of our Magic School Bus adventures!

The Truth about Bats
The Search for the Missing Bones
The Wild Whale Watch
Space Explorers
Twister Trouble
The Giant Germ
The Great Shark Escape
Penguin Puzzle
Dinosaur Detectives
Expedition Down Under
Insect Invaders
Amazing Magnetism
Polar Bear Patrol
Electric Storm
Voyage to the Volcano
Butterfly Battle
Food Chain Frenzy